P9-ELD-813

PLAY ME A STORY

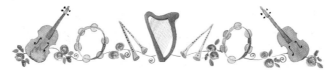

For my dearest Felicity and Ariane Adler, with love − N.A.
For my family, people, and pets − G.C.

Published in the United States in 1998 by The Millbrook Press, Inc.,
2 Old New Milford Road, Brookfield, Connecticut 06804

First published in Great Britain in 1997 by Barefoot Books,
PO Box 95 Kingswood Bristol BS15 5BH

Text copyright © 1997 by Naomi Adler
Illustrations copyright © 1997 by Greta Cencetti
The moral right of Naomi Adler as the author and
Greta Cencetti as the illustrator of this work has been asserted
1   3   5   4   2

All rights reserved. No part of this book may be reproduced in any form
or by any means, electronic or mechanical, including photocopying,
recording, or by any information storage and retrieval system, without
permission in writing from the publisher

This book has been printed on 100% acid-free paper
Printed in Hong Kong by South China Printing Company Ltd.

Library of Congress Cataloging-in-Publication Data

Adler, Naomi.
        Play me a story : nine tales about musical instruments /
[collected and] retold by Naomi Adler : illustrated by Greta Cencetti.
        p. cm. — (The barefoot book of musical tales)
        Contents: The Pied Piper of Hamlyn (German) —The horse
head fiddle (Mongolian) — Fairy music (Irish) — The dancing corn
maidens (Hopi) — The singing drum (African) — The singer and
the Dolphin (Greek) — The bewitched snake charmer (Indian) —
Didgeridoo magic (Australian aboriginal) — The painted balalaika
(Russian)
        Summary: A collection of tales originating in countries around the
        world and featuring a musical instrument native to each country.
        ISBN 0-7613-0401-0 (lib bdg)
1. Tales.   2. Music—Folklore. [1. Folklore.   2. Music—Folklore.]
I. Cencetti, Greta, ill.   II. Title.   III. Series.
PZ8.1.A24P1   1998
398.'.357—dc21   97—25708 CIP AC

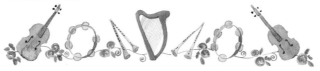

PLAY ME A STORY

NINE TALES ABOUT MUSICAL INSTRUMENTS

BY NAOMI ADLER
ILLUSTRATED BY GRETA CENCETTI

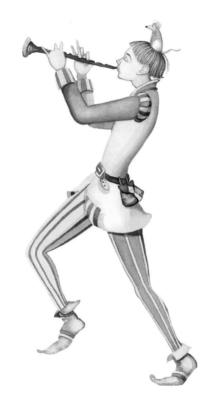

THE MILLBROOK PRESS
BROOKFIELD, CONNECTICUT

CONTENTS

THE PIED PIPER OF HAMELIN

~~~~~~~

GERMAN

Hundreds of years ago, a terrible thing happened in the town of Hamelin, in Germany. Hamelin was a beautiful and peaceful place, surrounded by fields and forests. A large hill called Koppelberg loomed over one side of the town, while the River Weiser flowed by the other side.

Hamelin had neat houses, fine schools, lofty churches, and excellent hospitals. It had a park full of trees and flowers, and there were lots of wonderful places for children to play. There were many shops, too: toy shops, candy shops, shoe shops and food shops. The people of Hamelin were hardworking, peace-loving and happy folk.

But one spring day, Hamelin was overrun with rats. There were rats absolutely everywhere. Soon there were hundreds and thousands of them, and the numbers grew every day. They ate the cheese out of the vats. Oh, they were such greedy rats! They nibbled the fruit and drank the milk, and they even licked the soup

6

from the cooks' ladles! They made their nests inside gentlemen's hats. And as if that wasn't bad enough, the noise the rats made was deafening.

Oh dear! The poor people of Hamelin were angry and hungry, thirsty and weary. They were at their wits' end. Finally they marched in a crowd to the town hall. They banged on the great wooden door, shouting, "We want the Mayor!"

The big fat Mayor and his councillors came sweeping out. The people of Hamelin were so angry that they shook their fists and cried, "We have had enough of these rats! Get rid of them now or else we will get rid of you!" Then they turned around and marched back to their homes muttering and grumbling to each other, shaking their heads and stamping their feet.

The Mayor sat down on his golden chair. He was in utter despair. He knew that he would have to get rid of all those rats or else find a new job. He thought and thought, he scratched his head and sighed. What could he do?

"Oh, for a trap! A trap! A trap!" he cried.

Just as he had uttered these words, what do you think happened? Upon his great wooden door he heard a gentle tap, tap, tap. Then the door swung open and in walked the strangest figure the Mayor had ever seen. He wore a strange long coat, half in yellow and half in red. And he himself was tall and thin with sharp blue eyes. Around his waist he wore a leather belt, into which was tucked a long, thin pipe. It was carved all around with mysterious signs and markings. His cap was long and pointed, with bells that jingled when he moved.

The Mayor and his council had never seen anyone so strange before. They wanted to send him away, but there was something about this man which both frightened and fascinated them.

"What do you want?" asked the Mayor.

The strange man stepped forward and said, "Please, your honor, I am the Pied Piper. If I am able by means of a secret charm to rid your town of rats, will you give me a thousand guilders?"

The Mayor was delighted: "My man! One thousand guilders, no, no! I will give you fifty thousand guilders if you will only rid my town of the rats."

Into the street the Piper stepped. Into the middle of the market square he leaped, the fat Mayor and his council running behind. The Piper smiled a little smile.

"No one can resist the magic music I play. Be it rat or bat, toad or viper, they will all follow the magic tune of the Pied Piper."

Then the Pied Piper laid his pipe upon his lips and played three shrill notes. At once things began to happen.

First, there was a grumbling and then a rumbling, as if an army were marching. Then there was a bustling and a rustling; then a creaking and a squeaking – and soon all of the rats came streaming out of the houses. There

were big rats, small rats, skinny rats, brawny rats, brown rats, black rats, grey rats and tawny rats. They came out of the windows and doors, down from the attics and up from the cellars, out of the houses, the churches and the hospitals. Soon the Pied Piper was surrounded by a sea of rats. Step by step, they followed him, dancing to the magic tune of his pipe.

When the Pied Piper came to the River Weiser, he stood on the bridge and played on his pipe, while all of the rats went tumbling into the river. One by one they were washed away by the swirling dark water. Every single rat was drowned. Well, not every single one. One rat managed to swim across the river without drowning and ran as fast as he could to Ratland to tell his tale.

No more rats!

You should have heard the people of Hamelin. They rang the church bells. They danced in the street and they sang at the top of their voices as they cleared their homes, blocked off the ratholes and destroyed their nests. They repaired all the damage until there wasn't a trace of a rat left.

Soon it seemed as if the rats of Hamelin had never been.

No more rats!

The Mayor was very pleased indeed, but most of all he was pleased with himself. He thought that he deserved a new cloak and a new gold chain as a reward. After all, it was thanks to his idea that the town had been rid of rats.

"Let's have a big party to celebrate our good fortune," he proclaimed in the middle of the market square. Then, all of a sudden, the Piper stepped out of the crowd.

"First, if you please, my thousand guilders," he said.

The Mayor turned pale, and so did his councillors. "Fancy asking for a thousand guilders just for playing a tune! You must think I'm mad to pay such a price! Take fifty guilders! That's all you'll be getting. We all know that the rats are dead. Take fifty and be gone! You can blow your pipe until you burst!"

"Very well," said the Piper, and he smiled his secret smile.

Once more he drew his pipe to his lips. This time he played a very different tune. This time his music was sweet and soft. And again, something amazing began to happen. There was a rustling and bustling as the children of Hamelin responded to the bewitching music. Then they came running, clapping, and

dancing all the while. No one could stop them. All the little boys and girls came

tripping and skipping after the wonderful music. But this time, when he reached

the River Weiser, the Pied Piper crossed by the wooden bridge, the children

dancing behind him, laughing and shouting.

The townsfolk tried to call them back but the children could only hear the

Piper's music. He led them right around to the other side of the town to where

Koppelberg, the large hill, stood.

The Mayor said, "He'll never cross that mighty peak. Never fear, our children

will be back soon."

But the Mayor had no idea of the Piper's power. All at once an opening

appeared in the side of the hill and the Piper danced through, with all the

children dancing and skipping behind him. When they were all inside, the cave

closed and the piping stopped.

Did I say all? No, not quite all. Just one child remained outside: a lame boy,

unable to keep up with his friends, had been left behind. As the days passed, he became sadder and sadder at the loss of his playmates. Life was dull without the other boys and girls.

Yet the lame boy never forgot the wondrous things the Piper's music had promised. It had spoken of a joyful land, with gushing waterfalls, brightly feathered birds and huge, fragrant flowers. He never forgot how the music had stopped and how he had found himself outside the cave, all alone. He searched and searched but found no way through the rocks and boulders into the magical land.

Of course, the people of the town were horrified. The Mayor sent messengers all over the world to find the lost children, but they soon realized that it was hopeless. The Piper and the children were gone forever.

Then the townsfolk commissioned a beautiful statue of the strange man playing his pipe, and around the base of the statue they wrote the story so that everyone would learn from it.

So you too should remember that if you make a promise, you must keep it. Or else!

THE HORSE-HEAD FIDDLE
~~~~~~~
MONGOLIAN

This is a sad story, but sometimes out of great sorrow something very beautiful is created.

Long, long ago in Mongolia there lived a small orphan boy named Suho. He dwelled in the Chahar district, where the people breed sheep, cattle, and horses. Suho's mother and father had died, so he lived with his grandmother in her yurt. A yurt is a big, round tent made out of thick sheep's wool. It is very cool in the summer and very warm in the winter, because it keeps out the sun, rain, and wind in turn.

Suho helped his grandmother with the meals and other household chores. But most of all he loved to take the sheep to graze on the hills.

While Suho took care of the sheep he encountered many wonderful people. He met shepherds and herdsmen, he met travelers and merchants, and they all told him stories. Some taught him how to make a flute and play it; others taught him how to make and play a fiddle. Suho began to sing the stories he had heard,

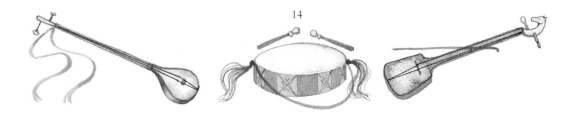

and when he played the fiddle, the sound was so beautiful that people from all over the district came to listen to him. Soon he became famous. He was known as Suho the Fiddle Player.

One night the most amazing thing happened. Suho did not return home from the hills at the usual time. His grandmother waited and waited. Then she became very worried and asked her neighbors if they had seen him, but no one knew where he was. They all wondered where the boy could be and hoped that nothing had happened to him.

The night was pitch-black when Suho finally appeared carrying in his arms a tiny white newborn foal.

"I found this little white foal all alone and helpless on the roadside," he said. "There was no sign of his mother anywhere. I was afraid that the wolves would get him so I brought him home to look after."

15

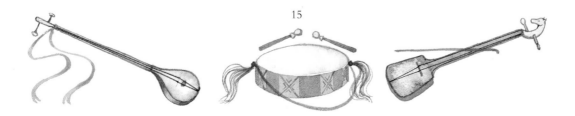

Suho had always dreamed of owning a horse. He also dreamed of becoming a champion horse rider and winning many races, but his grandmother was much too poor to buy him a horse. Now he had his very own little white horse.

Suho took great care of the horse and it grew to be strong and beautiful. Everyone admired and loved it, but of course Suho loved it most of all and was very grateful that his dream had come true.

Time passed. Suho and the horse grew up together. One night Suho was awoken by the sound of continuous neighing. He rushed out of the yurt and ran into the yard to find his white horse defending the sheep from a huge gray wolf. Suho drove the wolf away with a big stick. Then he hugged his exhausted horse, tenderly patting him and wiping away his sweat as he whispered, "Thank you for saving the sheep."

From that time on, the two of them were never separated, not even for a moment.

Suho then decided to make his other dream come true. He started to train and practice until he and the horse began to win all the races and tournaments held in the Chahar district.

Now the Khan of Mongolia had a very beautiful daughter, and he decided that she would be married to the best horse rider in the entire country. So he staged the greatest race ever to be held in Mongolia. It was to take place in the capital city, Ylaanbaatar, where the Khan lived in a magnificent palace. He announced that the winner of the race would marry the princess and one day become Khan of Mongolia. This news spread all over the country, and Suho's friends urged him to take part in the race.

On the day of the great race many strong, handsome young noblemen dressed in their best costumes came riding into the city. Suho took his place among them, on his magnificent white horse.

The signal was given for the race to start, and the horses were off, galloping with all the speed of a whirlwind. Faster than all the rest, the white horse was the first to reach the winning post. A tremendous cheer arose from the crowd: People clapped their hands and banged their drums. They danced and set off fireworks as they hailed the winner of the greatest horse race in all Mongolia.

The Khan proclaimed, "Call the rider of the white horse to come forward and claim his prize."

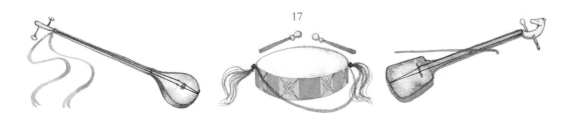

But when he saw that the winner was not a great nobleman, he withdrew his offer at once and instead ordered Suho to sell him the white horse for three silver coins.

Suho protested, "I have won the hand of your daughter. I did not come to sell my horse!"

The Khan was furious. "You rascal!" he thundered. "How dare a poor herdsman talk to me, the great Khan, like this? Seize him!"

So Suho was seized by the Khan's men and beaten soundly, while his horse was led away to the Khan's stables.

After the men had gone, Suho's friends rushed over to where he lay, bruised and bleeding, and carefully lifted him up. They then took him to his grandmother, who nursed him gently back to health in her yurt.

Meanwhile the beautiful white horse was led in triumph by the Khan at a special banquet he held in order to show off his new racehorse to his family and nobles. But when he tried to mount the horse, it reared up and threw him to the ground. Then it galloped away at full speed through the town.

In fury the Khan ordered his soldiers, "Catch it! And kill it!"

All this time the Khan's beautiful daughter, Ling, had been watching silently. She was horrified at how badly her father had treated Suho. She had often heard Suho sing and play his fiddle, and she thought him very brave and handsome. When she realized he had won the race, she was delighted at the prospect of marrying him. So now, when Ling saw the white horse in such distress, she sped through the crowds to open the city gates, and let the horse gallop to its freedom.

But the Khan's men, now mounted on their horses, were in hot pursuit and followed the white horse out of the city, shooting a shower of arrows at him. The poor horse was badly wounded, but it still managed to reach the yurt and tap at

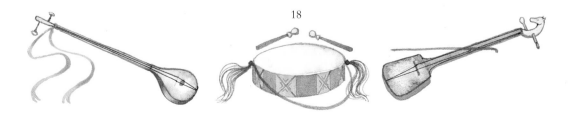

the door with its hoof. Suho's grandmother went outside to see who it was. She called out in amazement, "Suho, it's your white horse!"

Suho rushed out. He was so happy to see his beautiful horse. But his happiness turned to sorrow when he saw seven arrows piercing the body of his dearest friend. Gritting his teeth, Suho stifled his own cry of pain as he pulled out the arrows one by one. The poor horse died the next day, in the arms of his weeping friend.

Suho was not the only one to see the white horse die. Hiding behind a large tree was Ling. She had followed the horse all the way to Suho's home and she waited silently behind the tree, watching through her tears as the lovely animal died. Now Ling stepped out of her hiding place. She put her arm around Suho and said, "I am Ling, Princess of Mongolia. I have come to be your friend and to be your bride."

20

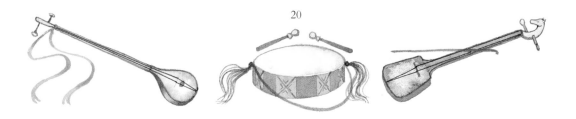

Suho looked up and saw the beautiful Ling. Her hair was piled on top of her head and covered with white and pink flowers. She had shiny red cheeks and dark sparkling eyes that looked like two drops of morning dew on a lotus leaf. Suho invited Ling to sit beside him, and together they grieved for the white horse.

In his sleep that night, Suho had a dream. In the dream the white horse appeared to him saying, "Make a fiddle out of my bones so that I will always be with you."

In the morning Suho made his new fiddle. Out of the bones of his dear friend he carved the head of a horse just like the head of his own white horse, and placed the horse's head on the upper part of the fiddle. He used the tendons for the strings of the fiddle and the hair from the horse's tail for the bowstrings.

Whenever Suho played on the horse-head fiddle, the memory of his dearest friend came back to him.

Then Ling and Suho were married and became traveling musicians. People flocked from all over Mongolia and China to hear their songs and listen to the sound of the horse-head fiddle. When at last the old Khan died, Ling and Suho became the rulers of Mongolia. Their palace was always full of music, laughter, and dancing. And that is why the Mongolian fiddle is always decorated with the head of a horse.

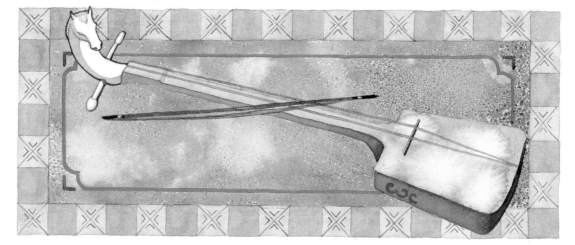

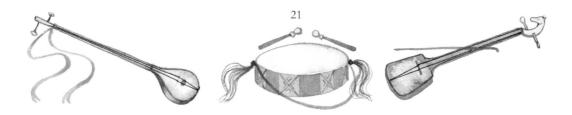

FAIRY MUSIC

~~~~~~~

IRISH

Once upon a time in the green, green emerald isle, where fairy folk live side by side with folk like you and me, there lived a poor widow and her son, Jack. They lived in a small, tumble-down house with their three cows. Jack and his mother loved these cows dearly, but times were hard and they had no money and no food. One day Jack's mother could stand it no longer.

"Jack," she said, "we must sell one of the cows. Go to the market and sell the white one."

And so, early in the morning, Jack and the white cow journeyed to the market at the nearby town.

When they reached the marketplace, Jack noticed a large crowd gathered in a circle. He pushed his way through the people to see what they were looking at. In the middle of the circle he saw a strange man dressed in a green coat and a green hat, holding a grasshopper in his hand. When the strange man put the grasshopper

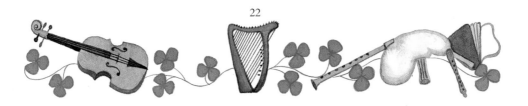

down in the street and began to whistle a tune, the grasshopper stood up on its hind legs, took a bow, and started to dance a jig.

No one had seen such a funny sight before. The crowd began to laugh and laugh and then, as if by magic, they too found themselves dancing and jigging, hopping and jumping, clapping and turning. On the market stalls the pots and pans, the reels and wheels all began to dance. Jack and the white cow were dancing too. Would you believe it – soon the entire town was dancing and jigging!

After a while, the strange man picked up the grasshopper and put it into his pocket. As if by magic, everything stopped dancing. The strange man then turned to Jack.

"Jack," he said, "how would you like to own this grasshopper?"

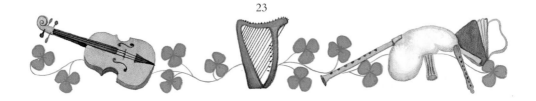

"Oh, yes please," said Jack. "I'd like that very much."

"Let's make a bargain," said the man. "I'll give you the grasshopper and you give me your white cow. That is the bargain, Jack."

"Done!" said Jack.

So it was that Jack made a bargain and went off home to his mother with the grasshopper in his pocket.

When Jack's mother saw him returning without the cow, she was overjoyed.

"Jack," she cried. "You have sold the white cow!"

"Yes, Mother, I have," said Jack.

"How much did you get for her?" she asked.

"Oh, Mother, I didn't get any money. I got something much better," replied Jack.

"Oh no, Jack, what have you done?" she cried.

"Wait a moment, Mother, and see for yourself," said Jack.

So saying, he took the grasshopper out of his pocket and placed it in the middle of the floor. Jack began to whistle a tune, and the grasshopper stood on its hind legs, took a bow, and started to dance a jig. He danced and danced, hopping and jumping, clapping and turning.

This was indeed a sight to behold. Jack's mother took one glance at the tiny creature and burst out laughing. She laughed and laughed until she thought that she would split in half. As if by magic, Jack and his mother found themselves dancing. The pots and pans, the cups and saucers, and even the tables and chairs also began to dance and jig all over the floor. Would you believe it – the entire house seemed to be hopping and jumping!

After a while, Jack picked up the grasshopper and put it into his pocket and, as if by magic, everybody and everything stopped dancing.

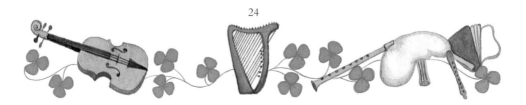

Jack's mother was still laughing, but when she came to her senses she was furious with Jack.

"You silly, foolish boy," she scolded. "There is no food and no money in the house! What are we to do? Go to the market, Jack, and sell the black cow."

And so it was that, early the next morning, Jack and the black cow journeyed to the market at the nearby town.

When they reached the marketplace, Jack again noticed a large crowd gathered in a circle. He pushed his way through the people to see what they were looking at. In the middle of the circle he saw the strange man dressed in his green coat and green hat, holding a mouse in his hand. When the man put the mouse down on the street and began to whistle a tune, the mouse stood up on its hind legs, took a bow, and started to dance a jig.

No one had seen such a funny sight before. The crowd began to laugh and laugh and then, as if by magic, they found themselves dancing and jigging, hopping and jumping, clapping and turning. On the market stalls the pots and pans, the reels and wheels all began to dance. Jack and the black cow were dancing too. Would you believe it – soon the entire town was dancing and jigging!

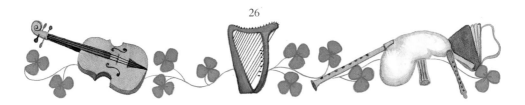

After a while, the strange man picked up the mouse and put it into his pocket. As if by magic, everything stopped dancing. The man then turned to Jack.

"Jack," he said, "how would you like to own this mouse?"

"Oh, yes please," said Jack. "I'd like that very much."

"Let's make a bargain," said the man. "I will give you the mouse and you give me your black cow. That is the bargain, Jack."

"Done!" said Jack.

So it was that Jack made another bargain and went off home to his mother with the mouse in his pocket.

When Jack's mother saw him returning without the black cow, she was overjoyed.

"Jack," she cried. "You have sold the black cow!"

"Yes, Mother, I have," said Jack.

"How much did you get for her?" she asked.

"Oh, Mother, I didn't get any money. I got something much better," replied Jack.

"Oh no, Jack, what have you done?" she cried.

"Wait a moment, Mother, and see for yourself," said Jack.

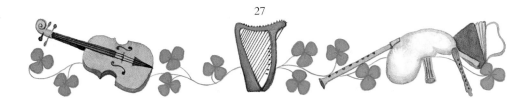

So saying, he took the grasshopper and the mouse out of his pocket and placed them in the middle of the floor. Jack began to whistle a tune, and the grasshopper and the mouse stood on their hind legs, took a bow, and started to dance a jig. They danced and danced, hopping and jumping, clapping and turning.

This was indeed a sight to behold. Jack's mother took one glance at the tiny creatures and burst out laughing. She laughed and laughed until she thought that she would split in half. As if by magic, Jack and his mother found themselves dancing. The pots and pans, the cups and saucers, and even the tables and chairs also began to dance and jig all over the floor. Would you believe it – the entire house seemed to be hopping and jumping!

After a while, Jack picked up the grasshopper and the mouse and put them into his pocket. As if by magic, everything stopped dancing. Jack's mother was still laughing but when she came to her senses she was furious with Jack.

"You silly, foolish boy," she scolded. "There is no food and no money in the house! What are we to do? Go to the market, Jack, and sell the black-and-white speckled cow."

And so it was that, early the next morning, Jack and the black-and-white speckled cow journeyed to the market at the nearby town. When they reached the marketplace, Jack once again noticed a large crowd gathered in a circle. He pushed his way through the people to see what they were looking at. In the middle of the circle he saw the strange man dressed in his green coat and green hat, holding a bumblebee and a wee harp in his hand. When the man put them down on the street and began to whistle a tune, the bumblebee started to play the wee harp.

No one had seen such a funny sight before. The crowd began to laugh and

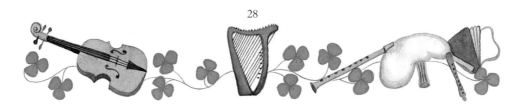

laugh and then, as if by magic, they found themselves dancing and jigging, hopping and jumping, clapping and turning. On the market stalls the pots and pans, the reels and wheels all began to dance. Jack and the black-and-white speckled cow were dancing too. Would you believe it – soon the entire town was dancing and jigging!

After a while, the tiny man picked up the bumblebee and the wee harp, put them into his pocket and, as if by magic, everything stopped dancing. The man then turned to Jack.

"Jack," he said, "how would you like to own the bumblebee and the wee harp?"

"Oh, yes please," said Jack. "I'd like that very much."

"Let's make a bargain," said the man. "I will give you the bumblebee and the wee harp and you give me your black-and-white speckled cow. That is the bargain, Jack."

"Done!" said Jack.

So it was that Jack made yet another bargain and went off home to his mother with the bumblebee and the wee harp in his pocket.

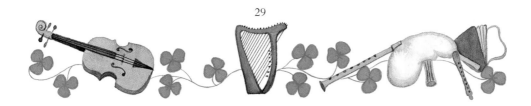

When Jack's mother saw him returning without the black-and-white speckled cow, she was overjoyed.

"Jack!" she cried. "You have sold the black-and-white speckled cow!"

"Yes, Mother, I have," said Jack.

"How much did you get for her?" she asked.

"Oh, Mother, I didn't get any money. I got something much better," replied Jack.

"Oh no, Jack, what have you done?" she cried.

"Wait a moment, Mother, and see for yourself," said Jack.

So saying, he took the grasshopper, the mouse, the bumblebee and the wee harp out of his pocket and placed them all in the middle of the floor. Jack began to whistle a tune, and the bumblebee began to play the wee harp, and the grasshopper and the mouse stood up on their hind legs, took a bow and started to dance a jig. They danced and danced, hopping and jumping, clapping and turning.

This was indeed a sight to behold. Jack's mother took one glance at the tiny creatures and burst out laughing. She laughed and laughed until she thought she would split in half. As if by magic, Jack and his mother found themselves dancing. The pots and pans, the cups and saucers, and even the tables and chairs all began

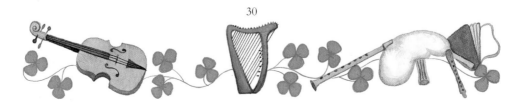

to dance and jig all over the floor. Would you believe it – the whole house seemed to be hopping and jumping!

After a while Jack picked up the grasshopper, the mouse, the bumblebee and the wee harp, put them into his pocket and, as if by magic, everything stopped dancing. Jack's mother was still laughing but when she came to her senses she was furious with Jack.

"You silly, foolish boy," she stormed. "There is no food and no money in the house! What are we to do? Jack, go out into the world and seek your fortune."

And so it was that, early the next morning, Jack went out into the world to seek his fortune. In his pocket were the grasshopper, the mouse, the bumblebee and the wee harp. As Jack walked down the road, thinking what a foolish and silly boy he had been, he met a tiny woman wearing a green coat and a green hat.

"Good morning to you, Jack," she said. "I know all about your bargains, my lad. Why don't you try your luck at the castle of the King of Ireland?"

"What do you mean?" asked Jack.

"Haven't you heard? The King of Ireland's daughter has not laughed for seven years and the king has promised to give her hand in marriage, together with all his kingdom, to the man who will make her laugh," said the tiny woman.

"If that is so," said Jack, "I must be off to the King of Ireland's castle."

So Jack set off, and when he reached the castle he found there was a ring of spikes around it and the heads of men topped every spike. You see, all those men who had tried to make the princess laugh but failed had had their heads chopped off!

Jack entered the castle. He called for the king and queen. He called for the princess and her maids. When a large crowd had gathered in a circle in the middle

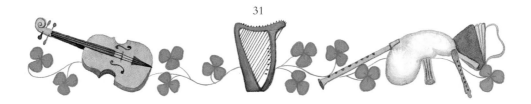

of the great hall, Jack placed the grasshopper, the mouse, the bumblebee, and the wee harp in the middle of the floor. He began to whistle a tune, and the bumblebee started to play the wee harp and the mouse and the grasshopper stood up on their hind legs, bowed to each other and started to dance a jig. They danced and danced, hopping and jumping, clapping and turning. In the castle kitchens the pots and pans and the cups and saucers and even the tables and chairs all began to dance. Would you believe it – soon the entire castle seemed to be hopping and jumping!

After a while, Jack picked up the bumblebee and the wee harp and the mouse and the grasshopper, put them into his pocket, and, as if by magic, everything stopped dancing.

The princess was still laughing when she came to her senses and said, "I have never seen anything so funny in all my life. Jack, I am more than willing to be your wife!"

Jack sent for his poor mother to attend their wedding. For the ceremony he washed his face and combed his hair and dressed in a suit made of silk. His mother could hardly recognize him.

"Jack, what have you done?" cried his mother, brimming over with joy.

"Wait a moment, Mother, and see for yourself," said Jack.

Would you believe it – Jack took out of his pocket the bumblebee and the wee harp, the mouse and the grasshopper, and placed them in the middle of the floor. He began to whistle a tune and … well, you know the rest.

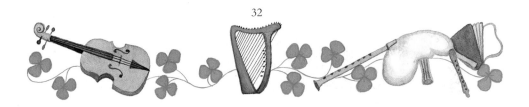

THE DANCING CORN MAIDENS

~~~~~~~

HOPI

In the beginning, the first people had only grass to eat. For many years they were very content with eating grass seeds, but there came a time when they no longer liked this poor diet. So they prayed to the sun and the moon, they prayed to the stars and the wind to send them better food. The spirits heard their prayers and asked the Great Pautiwa, father of the seed people, to send the beautiful corn maidens to help the first people to produce better food.

The corn maidens arrived dressed in exquisite white cloaks embroidered with all the colors of the rainbow. They danced amid the long grass for six days and six nights, and, as if by magic, new plants started to grow tall and strong. As the corn maidens danced they sprinkled star dust all over the plants, and the plants grew into radiant golden corn, shining and glowing in the sunlight.

The corn maidens stayed with the first people for a long time, teaching them how to take care of the corn, how to cook many different meals with it and how to

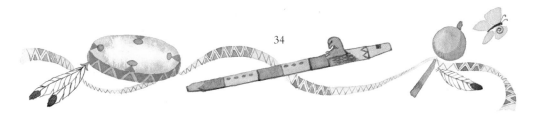

make beautiful clay pots to keep it fresh and safe. They were greatly respected and greatly loved, and together the first people and the corn maidens worked hard and grew healthy, strong corn that ripened each year into a rich and fruitful harvest.

But there came a time when the first people became lazy and forgot to honor and respect the corn maidens. They neglected the corn, they stopped gathering it as they had been taught, and they ceased storing it in the beautiful clay pots. They just left the corn to grow wild and rot on the ground. The corn maidens were very sad at what was happening. They warned the people, pleading with them to change their ways. But the people would not listen.

One day, one of the corn maidens, whose name was Golden Corn, said to her sisters, "It is time for us to leave this place. The first people no longer respect us. They no longer honor us. It is indeed sad, but we must leave now."

So the corn maidens left the village silently in the morning mist. Golden Corn led the way to brighten the path in front, and Black Corn followed last to

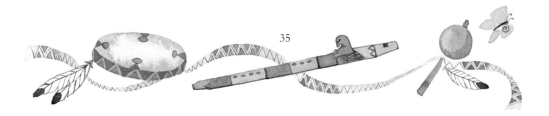

darken the path behind so that no one should see where they were going.

The corn maidens headed back to the father of the seed people, the Great Pautiwa. When they arrived at his camp they told him their sad story.

Pautiwa listened and answered thoughtfully, "The first people have behaved very badly and they deserve to be punished. So I will hide you until they realize their foolishness and want to change their careless ways."

And so it was that Pautiwa led the corn maidens to the south to a vast range of mountains. Following him, they climbed the highest of the mountains until they reached the shores of a lake.

Pautiwa stood at the edge of the water, stretched his arms up to the sky, and closed his eyes. There in front of the corn maidens he changed himself into a giant, snow-white duck and, gathering the corn maidens under his wings, he swam out into the deep, blue lake and vanished into the mist.

For a while the first people didn't notice that the corn maidens had vanished. They continued to behave carelessly, misusing and wasting the corn. Slowly, their supplies grew smaller, and, because they neglected the new plants, the crops became weaker until the time came when there was no food and the first people were hungry.

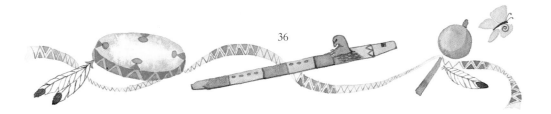

The Shaman and the other elders of the tribe called a council.

"We have been very foolish and uncaring, and now our people are dying of hunger," they said. "We must find the corn maidens and beg them to come back to us."

The Shaman decided to ask Great Eagle if he had seen where the corn maidens went. Eagle flew up high into the sky. He circled the north, west, south, and east. He scanned the mountains and searched the forests but found no trace of the corn maidens.

Eagle said, "The corn maidens are so well hidden that I couldn't find them, but why don't you ask Brother Buzzard? He can fly closer to the ground and will surely find them."

Brother Buzzard flew over the earth, skimming tops of trees and swooping down into every cave and crack in the rocks. But he too found no trace of the maidens.

As a last resort, the Shaman and the elders looked for Wise Owl, who knew everything that went on.

Wise Owl said, "There is only one way to find the corn maidens, and that is

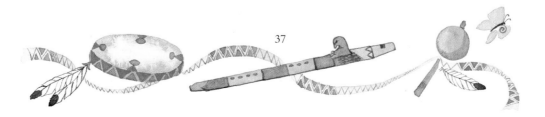

with music. It is music that calls the maidens into the fields. It is music that inspires them to dance and sing amid the corn. Paiyatuma plays the music, for it is he who created the flute and the drum. It is he who brings the dawn and scatters the dew drops to brighten the earth. Go to Paiyatuma."

The Shaman and the elders climbed the mountain that Wise Owl had pointed out to them and, there among the rocks, water was gushing from a spring, tumbling down the mountain as a bubbling brook. Through the sound of rushing water they heard exquisite music floating out of a dark cave. The opening of the cave was covered in mist and through the mist a brilliant rainbow arched overhead. Inside the dark cave Paiyatuma sat on a rock playing his flute, with his son beside him beating his drum. Paiyatuma wore a crown of enchanting flowers shining like dazzling jewels, and butterflies danced all around to the sound of his music.

"Help us, Paiyatuma, bringer of dawn," the Shaman pleaded. "Our corn maidens have left us and have taken all the corn with them. Please find them before our people die of starvation."

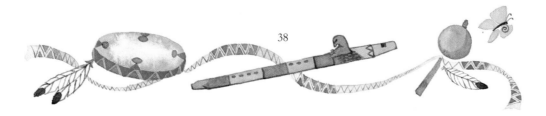

Paiyatuma smiled. "Go back to your people," he said. "The corn maidens cannot resist my music. When they hear it, they must dance their dance of corn. Have no fear: I will find them, wherever they are hidden, and I shall bring them back to you."

With dance and ritual, Paiyatuma prepared himself to find the corn maidens. He chanted to the sound of the drum beating, "Ho ho heya ho!" He stood still with his eyes closed and slowly turned, first to the east and then to the west. He chanted again, "Ho ho heya ho!" He turned to the north and then to the south. He stood still with his eyes closed. He knelt on the ground and placed his hands on the earth. He listened to the silence. He opened his eyes and knew exactly where to go.

Paiyatuma placed his flute to his lips, his son beat his drum, and they set off to the south, toward the vast range of mountains. With each step they took, flowers unfolded their petals and butterflies danced overhead. Their music filled the air and reached the lake where the corn maidens lay fast asleep under the soft, white wings of Pautiwa.

The maidens stirred and awoke. Pautiwa carried them to the edge of the lake and, opening his wings, set them ashore.

Paiyatuma came toward them and called out, "I have come to take you back to the first people. They need you. They have learned their lesson and beg your forgiveness."

The maidens turned to the father of the seed people, the Great Pautiwa. He threw off his feathered disguise and stood before them in his magnificent robes of white cotton, richly embroidered in all the colors of the rainbow.

"Yes, my sisters," he said. "Now is the time for you to return to the first people."

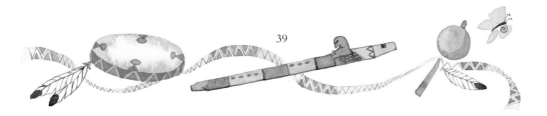

With Paiyatuma leading them, the corn maidens returned to the first people. Pautiwa followed, carrying a gourd filled with water from the lake.

When they entered the village, Pautiwa said to the first people, "I bring you this sacred water so that when you plant your corn, the rain will always come and you will have a good harvest."

Then Paiyatuma raised his flute to his lips and his son began to beat his drum, while the corn maidens started to dance through the streets. The first people wept for joy as they clapped their hands and danced behind the maidens.

As night fell, the music died away and the dancing stopped. Paiyatuma laid his flute at the feet of the Shaman, and his son laid his drum at the feet of the elders.

Paiyatuma spoke: "I shall come no more among you, but I leave you my flute and my drum. I leave you the secret of playing, so that you will always be able to make music for the dancing corn maidens."

With these words he and his son vanished into the darkness.

Pautiwa now spoke: "I will teach you the art of ceremony and chanting. You must promise to keep the customs of the corn maidens and learn their dances so that your corn will always grow and feed you."

With these words he too faded away into the morning mist and was seen no more.

Then it was the turn of the corn maidens to speak: "Let us bless the seeds and teach you once more how to care for the corn."

The Shaman and the elders began to play the music Paiyatuma had taught them. The corn maidens once more danced in the fields. Now the corn would grow strong and healthy and would ripen into a rich and fruitful harvest.

Then the corn maidens faded into the mist, but they promised always to return whenever the first people called them with their ceremonies, chanting, and music.

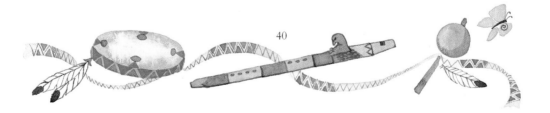

THE SINGING DRUM

~~~~~~~

SOUTH AFRICAN

There was once a girl known as the Tiny One. She was very beautiful but extremely small. Everyone in the village called her the Tiny One although she preferred to be called by her own name, Cuulu.

Despite being so tiny, Cuulu had a huge and powerful voice and she was a fine singer. In fact, she sang all the time. When she walked she sang, when she worked she sang, when she cooked she sang. Even in her dreams she sang. Cuulu was also a very gifted artist. She made baskets and mats, she created necklaces and bracelets. Even though she was so small, she was much sought after in marriage by the young men in the surrounding camps.

Sundu the Red Antelope Man lived not far away, just beyond the hills surrounding the village. Sundu was very fast, strong, and handsome. Sundu heard about Cuulu's beauty and her skills, and he wanted her as his wife.

So the Red Antelope Man came to the village and said to the elders, "I am

looking for a good wife. I have heard all about Cuulu the Tiny One and I would like to marry her."

Everyone in the village thought what a fine husband this fast, strong and handsome Red Antelope Man would make and they said, "Yes, the Tiny One is just the wife for you."

And so it was that the Red Antelope Man was invited to dance his antelope dance in front of Cuulu's hut. When she heard the beat of the drums, the Tiny One came out and sat down beside the elders. Sundu put on his magnificent antelope mask and he danced the dance of the antelope to the sound of the drums beating. When he had finished his dance he stood in front of Cuulu and asked her, "Will you marry me?"

She replied, "I will indeed marry you, but only if you bring me some delicious honey from the tallest tree in the forest."

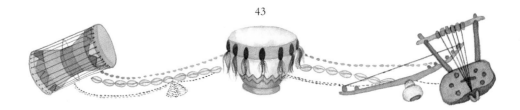

You see, at the very top of the tallest tree there was a nest of very special bees and they made the very finest honey. But no one had ever dared to climb up to the top of the tree and bring down the sweet, sweet nectar.

The Red Antelope Man tried his luck. He started to climb the tallest tree, but it was a long, long way up and, handsome and strong though he was, Sundu was unable to reach the honey.

When he returned to the village empty-handed, the elders said, "What sort of a man are you that you can't even get your wife-to-be some honey? You are no husband for our Cuulu. Be off with you!"

So Sundu went back to his camp where he told his sad story.

Boloko the Black Ape Man listened and said, "Now, I need a wife. I am clever and strong; I will surely win this girl." And he went straight to the village.

Boloko said to the elders, "I hear that the Tiny One is beautiful and skilled in many arts. I need a good wife and would like to marry Cuulu."

Everyone in the village thought what a fine husband this strong, clever Black Ape Man would make, and they said, "Yes, the Tiny One is just the wife for you."

Boloko the Black Ape Man was invited to dance his ape dance in front of Cuulu's hut. When she heard the drums she came out of her hut and sat down beside the elders. Boloko put on his magnificent ape mask and he danced the dance of the ape to the sound of the drums beating. When he had finished his dance he stood in front of Cuulu and asked her, "Will you marry me?"

She replied, "I will indeed marry you but only if you bring me some delicious honey from the tallest tree in the forest."

The Black Ape Man tried his luck. He started to climb the tallest tree, but it

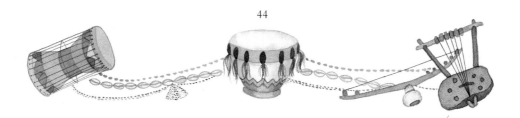

was a long, long way up, and, clever and strong though he was, Boloko was unable to reach the honey.

When he returned to the village empty-handed, the elders said, "What sort of a man are you that you can't even get your wife-to-be some honey? You are no husband for our Cuulu. Be off with you!"

So Boloko went back to his camp where he told his sad story.

Iblis the Yellow Hyena Man listened and said, "Now, I need a wife. I am cunning and strong; I will surely win this girl." And he went straight to the village.

Iblis said to the elders, "I hear that the Tiny One is beautiful and skilled in many arts. I need a good wife and would like to marry Cuulu."

Everyone in the village thought what a fine husband this strong, cunning Yellow Hyena Man would make, and they said, "Yes, the Tiny One is just the wife for you."

Iblis the Yellow Hyena Man was invited to dance his hyena dance in front of Cuulu's hut.

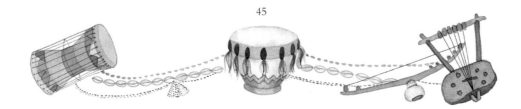

When she heard the beat of the drums, the Tiny One came out and sat down beside the elders. Iblis put on his magnificent hyena mask and he danced the dance of the hyena to the sound of the drums beating. When he had finished his dance he stood in front of Cuulu and asked, "Will you marry me?"

She replied, "I will indeed marry you but only if you bring me some delicious honey from the tallest tree in the forest."

The Yellow Hyena Man tried his luck. He started to climb the tallest tree in the forest, but it was a long, long way up, and, cunning and strong though he was, he was unable to reach the honey.

When he returned to the village empty-handed, the elders said, "What sort of a man are you, that you can't even get your wife-to-be some honey? You are no husband for our Cuulu. Be off with you!"

So Iblis went back to his camp and there he told his sad story.

Now Makatuwa the Gray Mouse Man also heard all about the Tiny One. When he heard that Sundu, Boloko, and Iblis had all failed to win her, he got up and said, "I am only a shy little Gray Mouse Man, but I will go and ask this girl to be my wife." Everyone in the camp laughed at Makatuwa, but off he went.

The villagers received him as they had received the others. Makatuwa put on his magnificent gray mouse mask and danced the dance of the mouse to the sound of the drums beating. He then said to Cuulu, "I will go and bring you some honey from the tallest tree in the forest."

The Gray Mouse Man tried his luck. He started to climb the tallest tree. It was a long, long way up, but, shy and small as he was, Makatuwa climbed up as quickly and as easily as could be. Working very hard, he dug out all the honey there was, brought it down, and took it back to the village.

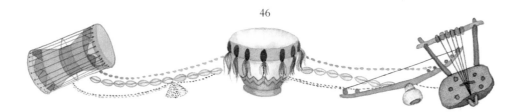

"Ah!" said the elders. "Here at last is someone who can fetch honey for his wife-to-be. Makatuwa the Gray Mouse Man is the husband for Cuulu the Tiny One."

And so it was arranged that Makatuwa and Cuulu would be married. Many things had to be prepared for the wedding. Cuulu had to make a wedding necklace out of shells and Makatuwa had to make a wedding headdress out of feathers and beads.

So Makatuwa went back to the camp to tell his happy story. Everyone cheered and blessed him – well, not quite everyone. Iblis the Yellow Hyena Man was so jealous that he decided to put a stop to the wedding.

The next day Cuulu went to the beach to gather beautiful shells for the wedding necklace. She was very happy and she sang a joyful wedding song as she collected the shells from the sand. Iblis had hidden himself behind a large rock, and when the girl passed by he pounced on her and stuffed her into his drum, saying, "Every time I beat my drum you will sing your beautiful songs."

And so it was that Cuulu the Tiny One disappeared. No one from her village knew what had happened to her. The villagers and the Gray Mouse Man looked everywhere for her but they never found the Tiny One. They were very sad to have lost such a gifted and loving member of their tribe, and Makatuwa was saddest of all to have lost his beloved bride.

Then Yellow Hyena Man changed his mask so that no one would ever recognize him. He set off, traveling far and wide with his singing drum. No one had ever heard such an unusual instrument before. No one had ever heard a drum with an exquisite voice singing such beautiful songs every time the drummer started to beat. Iblis was invited to perform with his singing drum at feasts and celebrations, at weddings and funerals. He became very famous and extremely wealthy.

After a few months, Iblis and his singing drum came to the Tiny One's village.

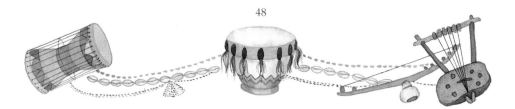

The elders had heard about the amazing singing drum and they invited him to entertain them. But when they heard the voice inside the drum they were not fooled. They recognized it as the voice of Cuulu the Tiny One.

The elders sent for Makatuwa the Gray Mouse Man. He gave Iblis a great deal of strong wine to drink. When Iblis was fast asleep, Makatuwa opened the drum, rescued Cuulu, and placed giant hornets inside the drum.

In the morning the Yellow Hyena Man woke up and traveled to the next village. When he beat his drum, instead of a beautiful voice coming out of it, a swarm of giant hornets flew out and stung Iblis all over. He ran to the river and jumped in to escape the stinging insects and was instantly transformed into a rock, which to this day is known as the Iblis Rock. No one dares to sit on it, though, because it is believed to have an evil spirit inside.

As for Cuulu the Tiny One and her beloved Makatuwa the Gray Mouse Man, they were married in splendor and joy, with feasting and dancing for three days and three nights. They lived happily in her village. Cuulu became famous for her exquisite singing and for making baskets and necklaces, while Makatuwa became a trader in the very special honey that he got from the tallest tree in the forest.

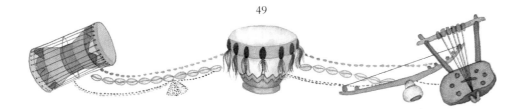

THE SINGER
AND THE DOLPHIN

~~~~~~~

GREEK

Long, long ago, in ancient Greece, lay the lovely island of Lesbos, on which lived many families and lots of children. One of these children was a very special boy named Arion. He was a beautiful child with curly black hair and piercing large brown eyes. Above all, Arion loved to sing and play the lyre. He could make music as no other child could; his voice was clear and sweet-sounding as no other child's sounded.

Arion's parents invited the best music teacher in Greece to instruct their gifted son. But Arion didn't like his lessons very much. He would often run off to the beach and jump into the sparkling, blue-green sea, playing and laughing, diving and dancing with his best friend – a dolphin.

Arion and the dolphin were inseparable companions. They would spend many hours together each day, singing and making the most beautiful sounds imaginable. The sea seemed to listen and dance with its waves to the wondrous music.

50

As Arion grew up into a handsome young man, he became the most famous minstrel in all Greece. He played the lyre more sweetly than anyone else and he composed the most enchanting songs and poems ever written. Everybody in Greece loved him and wanted to hear his magical music.

Arion was now seldom to be found in his beloved island of Lesbos. He spent his time traveling from one city to another, performing to merchants and nobles, to children and to parents. He traveled from one country to another, singing at the courts of kings and queens. But every once in a while he would return to Lesbos to greet his family and friends. And of course he would run to the beach and jump into the sparkling, blue-green sea, singing and laughing, diving and dancing with his beloved friend the dolphin.

Even on his travels, Arion never once forgot the dolphin. He composed a very lovely song about the mystical blue-green sea and its most ancient of travelers, the dolphins, and he would sing of his love for his special dolphin friend.

Then Arion was invited to sing at the court of the King of Corinth. Everyone came to his concerts there. Even the king's hunting dogs would come in and sit by Arion's side, listening to the sweet music. Even the fierce wolves from the forest would hear the music and come nearer to the palace grounds to hear more clearly the bewitching sound of the lyre. And even the great owls would come flapping down to perch in the dark trees by the palace, listening silently. There were many, many other listeners too, of which the people at the court knew nothing.

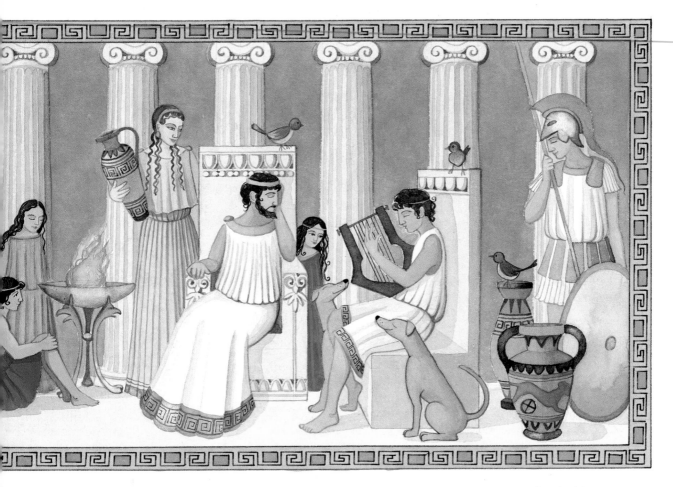

One day news reached Corinth that a musical contest was to be held in Palermo in Sicily. A huge chest of gold was to be the winner's prize. Poets and singers from all over the world set sail for Sicily, not so much for the treasure, but more for the glory that they hoped to gain.

Arion didn't care particularly for gold or for glory; he just loved to sing and make people happy. He also loved the excitement of traveling and meeting new people, learning all about their different lives, their hopes and dreams. The expedition to Sicily seemed a great opportunity for him.

So Arion also set sail for that island, having promised the King of Corinth that he would return after the contest. The king had become rather fond of the

young musician, so he did not wish to be parted from him for too long.

When the day of the contest came, Arion was so inspired by the beauty of Palermo, the capital of Sicily, and by the warmth of the people, that his heart opened out and he sang like an angel. The judges were overwhelmed by his talent, and he was awarded the first prize without any hesitation.

The people of Palermo wanted Arion to stay on in Sicily. The king even offered him a beautiful villa overlooking the sea and his youngest daughter's hand in marriage. But Arion longed to be back in Greece. Promising to return one day, he thanked his new friends and set sail for Corinth in a Greek ship.

Once Sicily disappeared over the horizon, the captain of the ship and his sailors, who were all very greedy, plotted to throw Arion overboard and to share his treasure among themselves. Quietly they tiptoed around Arion as he was resting in the sun up on deck. When they had completely surrounded him, the captain shouted, "Give us your chest of gold at once and then jump into the sea, or we'll push you in ourselves!"

Arion awoke with a start and pleaded with them: "You can gladly have all my gold but please spare my life!"

Yet his words were in vain.

"Into the sea you must go!" cried the captain. "That way no one will ever know what has become of you."

"I am not afraid to die," said Arion, "but, as one last wish, please let me dress in my minstrel's costume and sing one final song upon my lyre."

"Very well," said the captain. "But once the song is over, you must jump into the sea."

The captain and his sailors withdrew while Arion dressed in his full minstrel's costume. Despite their greed, they were all secretly delighted to be able to hear the last performance given by the most famous musician in all the world.

Arion began to sing a sweet song of his love of the island of Lesbos, of his wonderful childhood by the sea, and of his deep and abiding friendship with the dolphin.

All is sparkling, shining, shimmering
In the waters of the sea.
Green and mystical ancient traveller,
Emerald of the deep.
Dolphins are splashing, dancing, jumping
In the waters of the sea …

The song continued for a long time. Then, once it was over, Arion clenched the lyre close to his heart and leaped overboard. Without further ado, the sailors divided his treasure among themselves and continued on their way to Greece, inventing a story they would tell the King of Corinth.

But something amazing had happened while Arion was playing. His friend the dolphin heard the sweet music from afar. With great excitement he followed the sound until he reached Arion's ship and swam 'round and 'round it in sheer delight. At the very moment Arion jumped into the water, the dolphin caught the musician on his back and swam with him all the way back to Corinth.

When Arion arrived in Corinth he was brought before the king. But since the ship had not yet arrived, no one could believe his strange story. Besides, the captain was a good friend of the king. So poor Arion was locked up in prison.

However, a few days later the ship arrived at port in Corinth. The king at once summoned the captain and asked for news of Arion.

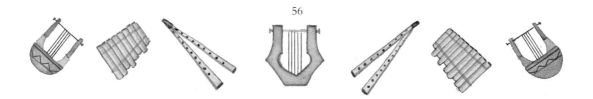

"We saw Arion in Sicily, your majesty," the captain answered. "He sang exquisitely and won the competition. The king invited him to live in Palermo and he has decided to remain there for the rest of his days, never to return to Greece."

The king then realized that Arion had spoken the truth and sent for him at once. Arion entered the great hall dressed in his minstrel's costume, just as he had been when he jumped into the sea. The captain and the sailors were so astonished and fearful when they saw he was alive that they confessed to their crime and were duly punished.

Arion's treasure was returned to him, and with it he built a music school for boys and girls to learn the art of singing, dancing, composing, and playing musical instruments. He also built a magnificent amphitheater where musicians, actors, and storytellers could perform to the delight and pleasure of the people.

Arion was hailed as a great hero, and in gratitude the king ordered a most beautiful statue to be erected in the harbor, showing Arion sitting on the back of a dolphin playing his lyre and singing his song. The statue can still be seen today so that all may remember the minstrel with his magical music and the dolphin who saved his life.

THE BEWITCHED SNAKE CHARMER

~~~~~~~

INDIAN

In times gone by, deep in the center of the kingdom of Rajasthan, there lived a powerful and mighty Rajah. He was very brave and very strong, yet at the same time very gentle and very kind to his three beautiful daughters whom he loved dearly.

The eldest daughter was Sundra, the middle daughter was Shanti, and the youngest was Sumitra. The two elder princesses were extremely jealous of Sumitra. They always complained that she was everyone's favorite princess.

Sumitra was indeed a very special girl. She loved to sing and dance; she loved walking through the city and meeting people. But most of all she loved to go to the market square, where she would watch the puppet shows and the acrobats and listen to the haunting music of the snake charmers.

Sumitra was full of joy and kindness, and everybody adored her quiet and gentle way. But Sundra and Shanti were always impatient with their younger sister. They felt that she was different from them, and this made them uneasy.

One day the Rajah announced that it was time for his daughters to be married.

He asked Sundra, "Whom would you like to marry, my child?"

Sundra replied, "Father, I would like to marry the richest prince in all of India."

"So be it, Sundra," agreed the Rajah.

He then turned to Shanti and asked, "Whom would you like to marry, my child?"

Shanti replied, "Father, I would like to marry the most handsome prince in all of India."

"So be it, Shanti," agreed the Rajah.

He then turned to Sumitra and asked, "Whom would you like to marry, my sweet child?"

"Dearest father, I would like to marry the man who makes the most charming music in all of India," Sumitra replied.

"So be it, my gentle Sumitra," agreed the Rajah.

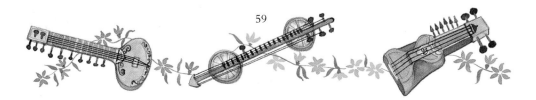

But Sundra and Shanti were furious that Sumitra had chosen a common musician. They believed that she was only saying this to make their father adore her even more. In their rage they both called out, "Put her to the test, Father! See if she really would marry a common music player. We're sure she doesn't really mean it."

What's more, the two sisters persuaded everyone in the palace to make the same demand. So the Rajah had no option but to put Sumitra to the test.

With great sadness he said, "My dearest Sumitra, go down to the marketplace at sunrise and find the musician who plays the most charming music in all of India. He shall be your husband."

Sumitra dressed in her finest red sari and put on her golden earrings and her sparkling necklace. She adorned her arms with bangles of every color and sprinkled herself with her favorite perfume. She was ready before sunrise.

Sumitra kissed her father farewell, and with tears in her eyes, she walked to the marketplace. She stepped gracefully through the hustle and bustle, the noise and smells, until she heard music in the distance. She continued in the direction of the lovely sound and soon found herself standing in front of a snake charmer playing the most exquisite tiktiri for a splendid cobra.

Sumitra was both charmed by the music and surprised at the sight she saw. The snake charmer was shabby and dirty, he was twisted and deformed, covered with warts and scabs. He was very ugly indeed. But his music was so enchanting that Sumitra soon forgot his ugliness. As she watched the cobra dance, she was spellbound by the intoxicating music. She also noticed a radiant light surrounding the ugly man sitting in the basket. Sumitra was aware that he was different from other men and rather special.

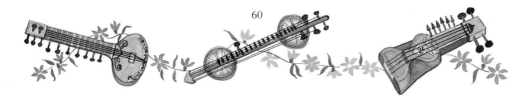

A large crowd gathered around, watching and listening in silent amazement and admiration. No one had ever seen this strange snake charmer before; no one had ever heard such magical music.

After a while the snake charmer played another tune. The cobra danced back into its painted gourd. The crippled man put the lid on top of the gourd to keep the snake safe inside. The crowd cheered and clapped. They loved the performance so much that they jumped up and down and stamped their feet. To show their gratitude some people threw money into the hat near the basket. But some horrid boys also came along and threw rotten mangoes at the poor snake charmer. They shouted cruel words about his disabled body, then they ran away.

The musician took no notice. With a peaceful smile on his face, he placed the painted gourd gently beside him and the exquisite tiktiri alongside it.

Sumitra watched silently. She was aware of how very beautiful the tiktiri was. It seemed rather strange to her that a deformed beggar would possess such an exquisite instrument, for the tiktiri was covered with chains of silver and sparkling gems. Indeed, it was an instrument fit for a prince.

Deep in thought, Sumitra stepped forward and said in a tiny voice, "I have come to be your wife. This is my destiny."

The snake charmer bowed his head low. He placed his hands together in front of him, as if praying. He accepted his young bride in silence and in devotion.

Sumitra bent down and picked up the painted gourd with the cobra inside. She placed it on her head and, as if she were merely carrying a feather, walked slowly out of the marketplace, through the city gate, down the dusty road, leaving her comfortable life at the palace, leaving her beloved father and jealous sisters. She walked into her new life with her husband the snake charmer.

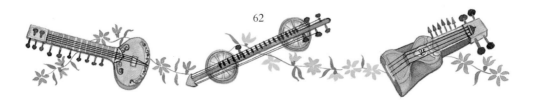

Together, Sumitra and the snake charmer traveled from village to village. Every day he charmed the cobra to perform the dance of enchantment, and Sumitra moved around them, performing her dance of joy, her dance of life.

After a few weeks, Sumitra's red sari was in tatters. She had sold all her jewelery. She no longer looked like a princess. Now she was a street performer, a dancer married to a snake charmer. Although very poor, with no roof over her head, Sumitra remained kind and gentle. Her beauty shone through despite her ragged sari, and everywhere she went she was adored by the crowds.

As the months passed, Sumitra grew to love her snake charmer. He was kind and gentle, and although he had difficulty in speaking, she learned to understand him. Between them grew a deep and loving friendship.

One very hot day Sumitra placed the gourd down under the shade of a large tree near the bank of a lovely lake.

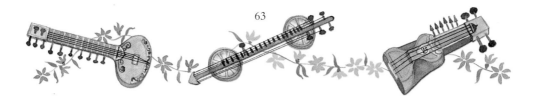

"I will go the next village and bring some food for us," she said. "You, my dearest husband, stay here and rest under the shade of the tree."

The snake charmer felt very sleepy in the heat of the day. He leaned back against the tree, gazing at the cool, still water. All of a sudden, he noticed an ugly crow flying over the lake. The bird dived into the water and, to his amazement, vanished. After a few moments, as if by magic, the bird emerged as a beautiful parrot with brilliant feathers. The snake charmer watched in disbelief as the parrot flew away.

"If the lake can transform an old crow into a magnificent parrot, I wonder if it could cure me?" the snake charmer thought to himself.

With these exciting thoughts he rolled himself down to the cool, still water, immersing himself completely except for the little finger of his left hand. He remained under water for a few moments and then, as if by magic, he emerged as a beautiful young man. His body was healed. Slowly, he walked back to the basket under the tree, sat down next to it, and waited for Sumitra to return.

At last Sumitra came back. She noticed the stranger sitting nearby and cried out, "Where is my husband? What have you done to him?"

The young man replied, "I am your husband."

Sumitra was very upset. "My husband is deformed and twisted, he cannot speak as eloquently as you. How can I believe what you say?"

The snake charmer placed his left hand in front of Sumitra.

"Do you recognize this little finger?" he asked.

Sumitra looked at the twisted finger covered in warts and scabs.

"This is truly the finger of my husband," she replied slowly. "Please tell me what happened while I was away?"

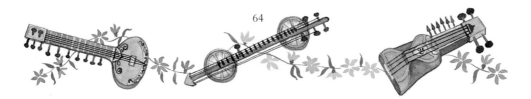

The snake charmer explained how he had seen the old crow dive into the water and emerge as a beautiful, multi-colored parrot.

"I decided to immerse my body in the magic lake and be healed," he continued. "You see, my beloved Sumitra, a long time ago I was a prince. An evil witch who hated my music put a magic spell on me. She changed me into a deformed beggar, until such a time that a princess would love me and bring me to a magic lake. You are that princess and this must be the magic lake."

So saying, he took Sumitra's hand and led her to the edge of the lake, immersed his little finger into the cool, still, water then lifted it out. The finger was healed.

The prince spoke: "Thank you, my dearest Sumitra for being so devoted and patient. Now it is time for me to take you to my palace and for you to live again in comfort and in royalty as you deserve."

So they journeyed back to the prince's kingdom, taking the cobra and the tiktiri with them. And they built a hospital on the bank of the magic lake so that many people could come and take the cure and be healed.

DIDGERIDOO MAGIC

~~~~~~~

AUSTRALIAN ABORIGINAL

In Yamminga times, when the Rainbow Snake spirit Ngalygod roamed the earth creating rivers, lakes, forests, and mountains, an evil giant spirit, Ngarri, also roamed the earth. She was as bright and as dazzling as the sun; it hurt the eyes just to catch a glimpse of her. Sometimes she looked like a giant woman covered with scabs and warts, as ugly as can be. Sometimes she looked like a spiral of light, and at other times she took the shape of a monster, stampeding through the bush screaming and shrieking. Every child was warned to beware of Ngarri!

One day in far off times there were two young Nimmamoo boys who went out into the forest in search of geerbaju honey. They followed the track of the wild bees. They laughed and told jokes. They jumped and swung on branches as they strayed ever deeper into the heart of the forest. When they had traced the bees to a particular tree, they would climb it. The higher they climbed, the louder became the busy humming of the bees inside the hollow trunk.

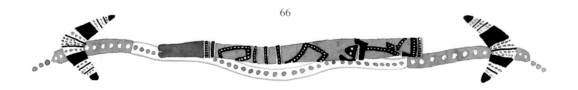

The Nimmamoo boys were just shinning down from one of the highest trees where they had found lots of sweet geerbaju honey, when suddenly out of nowhere they were bedazzled by such a bright light that their eyes were hurting from the blaze. They froze with fear, clinging to the tree trunk, as they realized this must be Ngarri. But there was no escape — she was coiled around the bottom of the tree trunk. With her long bony arm she reached out and snatched them up, stuffing them into a big wicker basket that she carried under her arm.

"Got you!" she shrieked. "I'm having you for my dinner."

"Help, help, someone please help us!" cried the boys. But it was no use — no one heard them. They were trapped in the clutches of Ngarri.

Ngarri ran like mad through the forest, shrieking and yelling. The boys inside the basket were thumped and bumped, hurled from side to side, bounced from bottom to top; they were bruised and scratched all over. Finally Ngarri arrived at her home in the hollow of a juniper tree.

Through the holes in the basket the boys could see her peeling back the bark of the tree, as if opening a door. Then she took each boy out of the basket and

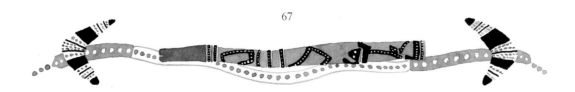

threw him into the tree, quickly covering the opening again with the bark.

Once inside the dark, gloomy juniper tree, the boys became even more afraid. They heard strange, sad sounds of children whimpering from deep within the pitch-black tree. The Nimmamoo boys began to hit the tree with their fists, crying, "Let us out, let us out!"

Then the strange shadow voices of the children drifted by, calling, "You are wasting your breath; no one will ever hear you."

"Who are you?" asked the boys.

"We were once boys like you. Ngarri has imprisoned us here and will one day eat us up just as she will eat you up too," replied the shadow voices.

Meanwhile Ngarri went hunting for some food for the boys. She brought back kangaroo, emu, and lizard to fatten up her prisoners so that they would all be nice and tasty for her dinner. The Nimmamoo boys became even more afraid. They knew that their turn was coming soon and they would also become shadow voices and then be eaten up by the terrifying Ngarri.

"We must escape," said one of the boys.

"But we will never be able to move that bark door," said the other boy.

"Let us be silent for a while and travel into dreamtime. The answer will surely be there," said the first boy.

So both boys sat down upon the roots of the tree. They took a deep breath, and in silence they sat for a long time just listening to the sound of their breathing. Then they entered dreamtime and a brilliant idea came to them.

The boys got up quietly and searched in the dark. They soon found a very good, strong branch, about as long as they were high. This branch had been hollowed out by termites long ago and would be ideal for their plan.

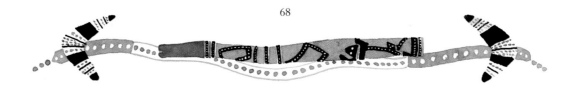

The first boy placed the branch against the bark door and began to blow into the hollow branch. He blew and he blew until he was puffed out.

"I'll try now," said the second boy. He began to blow and to blow. On and on he blew, circulating the air through his nose and mouth so that he could breathe and blow at the same time.

After a while, a strange, deep sound came out from within the hollow branch. The sound grew louder and louder and deeper and deeper. The boys felt as if the sound were vibrating out of the belly of Mother Earth.

The tree began to shake. They felt the vibration through their whole bodies. Suddenly the bark door fell away and the Nimmamoo boys and all the shadow voices tumbled out of the tree.

"Quick!" cried the shadow voices. "We must run like the wind – Ngarri will soon be after us."

They all ran as fast as their legs could carry them. They ran like the wind as if a magic force were guiding them. They ran through the Googoorewon (the forest). They ran on and on, never stopping, not even once, until they reached their camp.

The Nimmamoo boys cried out to their elders: "Ngarri is after us. Help us, please help us! Do something at once or she'll take us back!"

Quickly they explained what had happened to them and to the shadow voices and how they had escaped using the deep, vibrating sound made by the hollow branch. They handed the branch to the elders.

The head of the camp took the branch and began to blow into it as the boys had done, circulating the air through his nose and mouth so that he could breathe and blow at the same time. Suddenly the same deep, vibrating sound came forth, the earth began to shake, and the trees began to tremble.

70

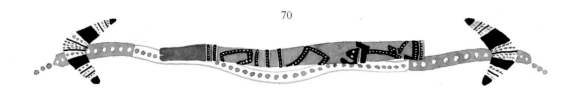

The shadow voices had been right: Ngarri flew into a terrible rage when she discovered her tree was open and the boys had escaped. She very soon found their footprints in the dust and their smell in the wind, and she took off like a whirlwind after them.

When she reached the camp she heard the deep, penetrating sound; she felt the earth vibrating; she felt the vibrations run through her body; she froze to the ground and could go no farther. Magically, the sound had created an invisible wall that encircled the camp. Ngarri screamed and shrieked; she yelled and growled; she hit and kicked the invisible wall, but no matter how hard she tried she could not break through it. Exhausted, she finally admitted defeat and returned to her juniper tree in a fury.

The Nimmamoo boys were now heroes, and the hollow branch they used to defeat Ngarri became known as the didgeridoo.

The boys grew up to become mighty hunters, and they painted scenes from their adventures onto their didgeridoo. In the evenings they would sit around the campfire, play the didgeridoo, and tell to all assembled the stories of their great adventures, safe in the knowledge that Ngarri could never get them again.

THE PAINTED BALALAIKA
~~~~~~~
RUSSIAN

Once upon a time, there lived an old man and an old woman who had three daughters. The two elder daughters wore brightly flowered dresses and gilded beads and boots with high heels. But the youngest daughter, Mashenka, wore gowns as dark and dull as her eyes were light and bright. Her one adornment was her hair, which fell to the ground in a long golden plait and brushed the flowers in her path as she walked.

The elder daughters were lazy and sat about doing nothing, like two grand ladies, but Mashenka was always busy around the house and in the fields and garden. She would weed the vegetables and chop firewood; she would milk the cows and feed the ducks. Her sisters would order her about and make her do their chores for them, but she never complained.

And so life went on, until one day the old man took the summer hay to market. Before he left, he promised to bring each of his daughters a gift and asked them what each would like.

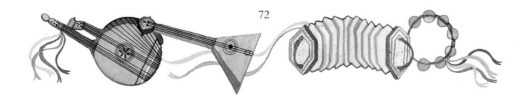

The first daughter said, "Buy me a necklace of silver and gold."

The second daughter said, "Buy me a length of red velvet."

But Mashenka said nothing. The old man went up to her and asked her gently, "What shall I buy for you, Mashenka, my child?"

"Well, Father dear, I would like a balalaika painted all over with the flowers and animals, people and houses of my beloved Russia."

Whether the old man went far or near, and whether he was long away or not, no one knows, but he sold his hay and brought each of his daughters their desired gifts.

The two elder sisters were overjoyed with their gifts but laughed when they saw Mashenka's balalaika, even though it was beautifully painted with flowers and trees, animals and birds, houses and people.

Mashenka sat down in a corner of the hut. Remembering the song that an old beggar woman had taught her in exchange for a loaf of bread, she began to play and sing:

> *Play a tune, a magic tune, sing a song, a magic song.*
> *Show me towns and villages, show me forests and seas,*

Show me mountains high as the blue, blue sky,
Show me all of Russia, my own dear land.

All of a sudden there came a ringing of bells and the whole hut was ablaze with light. The paintings on the balalaika began to move and change, and there appeared towns and vales, hills and dales, soldiers in the fields with swords and shields, ships on the seas, and mountains as high as the blue, blue sky, where the bright sun chases the pale crescent moon and the stars dance all night.

The elder sisters turned green with envy. Their only thought was to find a way of getting the balalaika from Mashenka. But Mashenka would not part with her beloved instrument and she went on playing and singing every evening.

One day the elder sisters could bear it no longer, so they decided to lure her into the forest.

"Come, sweet sister," they said. "Let us go gathering berries in the forest. We'll bring back some wild strawberries for Mother and Father."

They went together deep into the forest, but found no berries. Mashenka sat down against a tree. She began to play and sing:

74

Play a tune, a magic tune, sing a song, a magic song.
Show me where the wild strawberries grow.

All at once there was a ringing of bells and the forest was ablaze with light. The paintings on the balalaika began to move and change and all the secret nooks of the forest appeared, the glades where the wild strawberries grew, the damp corners where mushrooms flourished and the hidden places where springs gushed forth.

Mashenka's spiteful sisters looked on and were filled with such envy that their hearts froze. In their madness they beat Mashenka until she died. They buried her body underneath a silver birch tree and took the painted balalaika for themselves. It was evening by the time they reached home, bringing baskets full of mushrooms and berries.

"Mashenka ran away from us and she got lost," they told their parents. "We looked for her all over the forest but we couldn't find her. The wolves must have eaten her up."

The mother burst into tears and screamed and yelled for her beloved daughter. But the father said, "Give me the balalaika. It will surely show us where she is."

75

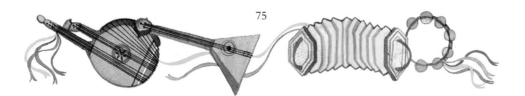

The sisters turned cold with fear but did as their father bade. He played and he sang, but the paintings on the balalaika did not move and did not change. Full of sadness, the old man put the painted balalaika away in a cupboard.

Now it so happened that at that very moment a young shepherd was out in the forest, and he came upon the silver birch tree with a freshly heaped mound of turf beneath it. Seeing some long slender reeds, the shepherd cut himself one and made a pipe out of it. No sooner had the pipe touched his lips than it began to play and sing of its own accord:

> *Play, pipe, play for the shepherd to hear*
> *How my sisters killed me just for the sake of my painted balalaika.*

The shepherd was frightened and ran back to the village. He told the villagers what the pipe had said and they gasped in horror. They all ran to the hut of the old man and his wife and explained what had happened.

"Take us to where you cut the reed, good shepherd," said Mashenka's father.

So the shepherd led them to the mound in the forest. They dug it up and there lay Mashenka, more beautiful than ever. The old man put the pipe to his lips and it began to play and sing of its own accord:

> *Play, pipe, play for my father to hear.*
> *By my sisters in the forest I was slain.*
> *Play, pipe, play for my father to hear.*
> *If you wish to see me alive and well,*
> *Fetch some healing water from the Tsar of Russia's well.*

76

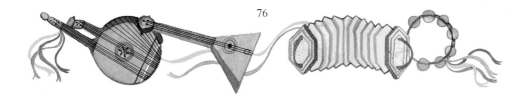

At this, Mashenka's two wicked sisters fell to their knees and confessed their crime. They were put away behind iron bars to await the Tsar's orders.

Meanwhile the old man set out to the Tsar's city to fetch the healing water. At the palace he was led before the Tsar himself. The old man bowed to the ground and told the Tsar all about Mashenka.

The Tsar listened attentively and said, "Old man, take some healing water from my well and when your daughter comes back to life, bring her and her two elder sisters to me. Make sure Mashenka brings the painted balalaika with her."

The old man was overjoyed. He bowed to the ground several times and took a jar of the healing water home with him. No sooner had he sprinkled the healing water over Mashenka than she came back to life and gave her father a tender hug.

The old man took his three daughters to the Tsar's city. When they arrived at the palace, they were all led before the Tsar. Mashenka stood before him – lovely as a spring flower, her eyes bright as the rays of the sun, her face beautiful as the sky at dawn, and tears like the purest of pearls rolled down her cheeks.

The Tsar gave her a gentle hug and said, "Welcome to my palace, dearest Mashenka. I have heard much about your painted balalaika. Please do me the honor of playing it."

Mashenka began to play and sing upon her painted balalaika:

> *Play a tune, a magic tune,*
> *Sing a song, a magic song.*

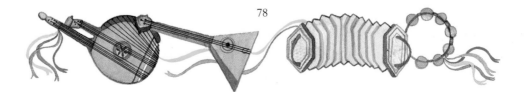

All of a sudden there came a ringing of bells and the whole palace was ablaze with light. The paintings on the balalaika began to move and change, and there appeared towns and vales, hills and dales, soldiers in the fields with swords and shields, ships on the seas, and mountains as high as the blue, blue sky where the bright sun chases the pale crescent moon and the stars dance all night.

Mashenka fell to her knees and begged the Tsar, "Take my painted balalaika, only please pardon my sisters. Do not put them to death."

The Tsar, lifting her up from her knees, replied, "Mashenka, your balalaika is magic, but your heart is pure gold. Will you be my own dear wife and Tsarina of Russia? As for your sisters, I shall pardon them, but only because you wish it."

Mashenka received her parents' blessing and she was married to the Tsar with great rejoicing and feasting. The palace was ablaze with light and the crowds cheered and danced. Even the wicked sisters relented, and they and their parents lived at the palace happily for many years.

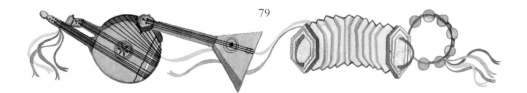

SOURCES FOR THE STORIES

Ever since I was a small child I have loved stories. At first it was my father and grandfather who told me myths, legends, and fairytales. When I grew up I became a storyteller myself, and now I collect stories from many people around the world.

THE PIED PIPER OF HAMELIN (GERMAN)

I read the Robert Browning poem of the Pied Piper when I was in school and I liked it very much. Many years later, when I ran my first shadow puppet workshop at the Polka Theatre, I used this story.

THE HORSE-HEAD FIDDLE (MONGOLIAN)

I once saw a film about Mongolian horses and the life of the herdsmen and women of that country. It was during the film that a story was told about the horse-head fiddle, and it was this that inspired me to write the story in this collection.

FAIRY MUSIC (IRISH)

I was sitting in a pub in Kilburn, Ireland, drinking a pint of Guinness. I was deep in thought when an Irishman named Pat sat down next to me. He said that I was looking rather sad and he could tell me a funny story to cheer me up. Pat then told me the story "Fairy Music," and I felt much better.

THE DANCING CORN MAIDENS (HOPI)

This story was passed on to me by Floating Eagle Feather, a Mayan Native American storyteller, when we met in London in 1984. A few years later, my brother's wife, Kay, came to visit me from the U.S. and brought me a beautiful Hopi necklace, which inspired me to tell this story. I have since told the story to many children, and I always wear the necklace when I am telling it.

THE SINGING DRUM (SOUTH AFRICAN)

At the time that Nelson Mandela was freed from prison in 1990, I attended an African drumming workshop to celebrate this great event. During the workshop we shared stories about captivity and freedom. "The Singing Drum" was one of the stories told, and I have been telling it ever since.

THE SINGER AND THE DOLPHIN (GREEK)

Margaret Button, a wonderful friend and storyteller, told me this story. She was an expert on Greek myths, and we shared a love of stories and of dolphins. Margaret passed on to me this story for my collection of stories about dolphins. It was Rod Wilson, a musician and another friend of mine, who wrote the delightful dolphin song that Arion sings before he jumps into the sea.

THE BEWITCHED SNAKE CHARMER (INDIAN)

A troupe of puppeteers from Rajasthan came to London to perform at the Aditi exhibition of Indian art, held at the Barbican Centre in 1982. One of the stories they performed was "The Bewitched Snake Charmer." When I told the puppeteers that I also was a puppeteer and storyteller, they gave me as a present all the puppets that they used for performing the story. The puppets are still hanging in my home, and I often use them to tell this story.

DIDGERIDOO MAGIC (AUSTRALIAN ABORIGINAL)

In 1983 an exhibition of Aboriginal paintings was held at the Hayward Gallery in London. As I was looking at the paintings, I met Wendy Watson, an Aboriginal storyteller. We sat under one of the paintings and she told me a number of stories from her people. "Didgeridoo Magic" was one of these stories.

THE PAINTED BALALAIKA (RUSSIAN)

During 1992, I was invited to run workshops and tell stories in Russia. My interpreter was an amazing woman called Margareta Sergiyenko. She took me to an enchanting children's park where I noticed a statue of a girl playing a balalaika. As we stood beside this charming statue, Margareta told me the story of the painted balalaika.

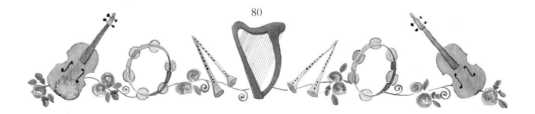